# Eagle Owl's Plastic Plight

## Covid-19, A Cry from Nature

Written by **Ismail Gani**
Inspired by a true story
Illustrated by **Ammie Miske**

AuthorHouse™ UK
1663 Liberty Drive
Bloomington, IN 47403  USA
www.authorhouse.co.uk
Phone: 0800 047 8203 (Domestic TFN)
+44 1908 723714 (International)

This book is printed on acid-free paper.

ISBN: 978-1-7283-5290-9 (sc)
978-1-7283-5289-3 (e)

Print information available on the last page.

Published by AuthorHouse  05/18/2020

**author**HOUSE®

# Eagle Owl's Plastic Plight

"Cherish the natural world, because you're a
part of it and you depend on it."

Sir David Attenborough

For the world and it's living things

# Foreword

"Sweet are the uses of adversity,
Which, like the toad, ugly and venomous,
Wears yet a precious jewel in his head;
And this our life, exempt from public haunt,
Finds tongues in trees, books in the running brooks,
Sermons in stones, and good in everything."

As You Like It, William Shakespeare

Adversity can have its benefits. Even an ugly, poisonous creature like a toad wears a precious gem inside its head. In this life, even in the midst of a global pandemic like the current coronavirus outbreak, far away from our normal world, we can hear the language of the trees, read the books in the running streams, hear sermons in the stones, and discover God and good in everything.

We should not be disheartened by this challenge and we should look at it positively. Just like soccer brings the world together, coronavirus has united the world. There is no talk of war and there is no talk of guns. Covid-19 has brought human beings together and has shown us that we are one. We are more similar than we had ever imagined and we have the same hopes and fears.

Like passionate Rory cleaned up the polluted soccer field and artistically created bird nests and owl homes from the plastic, human beings are sure to find a solution and clean up the pollution that they have created in the world. After the game of soccer and the virus is over, we will clean up the mess that we have created on Earth's large playing field together. We will rebuild a new world scoring 2 goals in one: a clean earth and giving back a home to our beloved animal friends.

Dr Khalid Ismail

# Acknowledgments

I would like to thank my parents Rehan and Kaamila, and my siblings for the endless support that they gave me during the publishing of my book. Also a huge thank you to my grandparents, Dr Khalid and Khadija Ismail from Polokwane, who have encouraged me to remain positive in all situations. They have inspired me to have a growth mindset with regard to the changing of my learning environments these past few months. I would like to thank our heroic and respectable president Mr Cyril Ramaphosa who has responded swiftly and responsibly to the lockdown, making personal sacrifices for the people of South Africa. His composure, humble character and positive attitude during the Covid-19 pandemic is admirable. Specials thanks to the Directors of Owl Rescue Centre, Brendan and Danelle Murray for inspiring me to get involved with owl and bird life conservation and for making the publication of my book possible.

Ismail Gani

Famous South African Birds

Eagle Owl

Blue crane

Ground Hornbill

Secretary Bird

The entire stadium erupted into a series of applause and cheers. Orange confetti and fireworks rained down from the roof of Soccer City Stadium in Johannesburg, onto the thousands of fans sitting below. Everyone was cheering and the buzzing sound of vuvuzelas filled the air. The referee had just blown the whistle. Bafana Bafana had won the cup, becoming the new champions. Thousands of orange helium balloons escaped from the orange calabash, decorating the Sowetan sky and celebrating Bafana Bafana's victory. Suddenly Rory, was awoken from his daydream.

It was just a daydream again! Rory was sitting on a seat of an empty Soccer City Stadium. How he longed to hear once again the sounds of human beings laughing and cheering. The coronavirus Covid-19 lockdown seemed surreal. There was no one in the stadium, except Rory. It was in silence. He sat in the stands all alone. He was 13 years old and his full name was Rory Maloko.

Why was he alone at Soccer City Stadium in Johannesburg? The truth was that it was his home. Rory's father had left their family when he was a child. He lived with his mother who was a cleaner at the Stadium. She was responsible for mopping up the large amounts of litter left behind by the fans after each match. The last match had been played a week before the lockdown. There was so much litter that Rory and his mum had not managed to pick everything up as yet. It seemed impossible to pick up all the plastic balloons, confetti, packets and plastic bottles. If they worked together, they knew that it would eventually get done. Time seemed to move slower during the lockdown and there was more time to reflect.

Rory loved his two roomed house behind the stadium, as it had a magnificent view of the stadium through the only window in the house. He decorated his walls with pictures of his favourite soccer players and soccer teams. Before the lockdown, he would often proudly bring friends home after school to see the stadium. Now without attending school, days seemed so long and things seemed so different. He was concerned about his education during the lockdown, the food price increase and his mum's job.

Rory stood up from his seat in the stadium where he had stopped to take a rest. He walked around the stadium to finish up the job. It was getting dark and the sun was setting. Rory loved to keep aside certain types of plastic, from the litter, that he could reuse for his own personal use. He would often reuse the plastic to build toys and gadgets to play with.

As he started his collection, he noticed unusual activity of birdlife in the air and on the field. It seemed that the absence of sound pollution, was an invitation to the birds and animals to enter the stadium. His eye caught glimpse of a gigantic bird flying above him in the dark stadium. As Rory continued to watch this unusually awkward bird above the field in the stadium, he realized that something seemed strange. The bird was struggling to keep control of its flight. It was flapping its wings, trying to regain control of itself.

The bird began to descend fast and was heading straight towards the goal post. It started flapping its wings frantically trying to lift itself back up, but it couldn't. The bird pounded straight into the goal post nets and got tangled within it. Rory ran to help it. "Poor bird!" he exclaimed. As he got closer, he realized that the bird was actually a large, brown Spotted Eagle Owl. The owl had a pale face with two round dazzling yellow eyes. He noticed that something orange was also tangled around its wing.

As he got closer, he realized that it was a piece of one of the orange helium balloons that was released during the celebrations. Rory looked into the owl's sad eyes and could almost see the fear and pain that it was experiencing. He decided to help the owl.

The owl was so entangled that it couldn't move. He beckoned his mum to come over. She asked some workers from the area if they could help too. They practiced social distancing and wore cloth masks.

They started by untangling the owl from the goal post net. The owl was so patient. They had to be extra gentle because the owl was very frightened. Rory gently comforted the owl as they went along. "It's going to be alright," he said. They had to cut parts of the goal post net. They first cut the longer parts and then the shorter parts off from the owl. Finally the owl started to come loose from all the tangled net. They then raised the owl into the air. The difficult part was to untie the huge knot of orange plastic balloon from under its wing. They had to gently untie the piece that went around its neck.

Rory covered the owl's head to keep it calm. They cut every bit of balloon and net that was still left. The plastic had dug right into its feathers. They had to be careful where they cut. He was tangled in the string and plastic. They continued cutting. The owl stayed absolutely still while they worked, almost as if it trusted and had confidence in them. Big pieces of plastic and string came off. They needed to be slow and steady. Eventually the rest of the small plastic pieces and string fell off. The owl was free!

Once every bit of net and balloon was off, Rory placed the owl onto the floor hoping it would fly. It seemed that although the owl was free from the tangle, it needed some rest. Rory decided to look after it until it recovered. Rory named the owl Percy, after his favourite Bafana Bafana soccer player. Rory gave Percy some food and water. Percy was very thirsty. South Africa was experiencing a terrible drought. Rory thought about how global warming was causing drought and impacting these birds. He wished that he could create an awareness about the effects of deforestation and human activity on these birds.

Over the next few days, Rory began to build an owl house from the plastic litter that he had collected. Rory made a large bird house where Percy could stay whilst he recovered. This was by far one of the best things that Rory had ever built from recycled plastic. He mounted the owl house just outside the stadium in a covert high area, ideally camouflaged.

Over the next week, Rory went daily to the owl house, taking food and water for Percy. He used his creative skills to make new items from recycled material. "If I could make more for selling, mum would regain her income," he thought. He made containers in which the owl could drink water and eat food. Other birds also came to drink water from the oasis that Rory had so cleverly created. He shared some of his food with the birds, despite him having his own food shortage.

One evening, as he got to the owl house, Percy was gone. He looked up and soaring in the night sky above, was Percy. Percy had learnt to fly again! Percy gave a loud cry as if to say, "Thank You for saving me!". The nocturnal bird then flew off into the darkness.

Facts about the effects of human activity on Spotted Eagle Owls.

The Spotted Eagle Owl is also known as the African Eagle Owl.

They are nocturnal. They roost during the day and are active during the night. At sunset they fly out to hunt. Although they are capable of looking after themselves and they have adapted to **human activity** in the environment, too many owls die unnecessarily because of **human activity**. They die from eating rats that have been poisoned by pesticides. They are killed by cars on the roads at night. They fly into barbed wire on fences. Owls are often killed by people who fear owls or by people who use their body parts in traditional medicine.

Facts about the harmful effects of plastic pollution on birdlife.

The ***human activity*** of plastic production has become a huge problem globally. Plastic is found in the guts of 90 percent of seabirds. The rate is growing fast! Plastic that is found inside birds include plastic bags and tags, straws, plastic bottles and tops and synthetic fibre from clothing. Plastic is broken down into tiny plastic bits by the sun and waves. Some seabirds eat so much plastic, that there is little room left in their gut for food, which affects their body weight and health. Sharp-edged plastics also kill birds by punching holes into their internal organs.

Facts on how global warming and climate change causes drought and the impact on birdlife.

Industrialization and deforestation due to ***human activity***, has been one of the main causes of global warming and climate change, because of gas emissions and the greenhouse effect. While droughts can have different causes, most scientists believe that the recent droughts which are being experienced are due to global warming and climate change. Raised air temperatures cause more moisture evaporating from water bodies, resulting in drought. The loss of habitat due to deforestation and the drought due to global warming have both had a huge impact on birdlife.

Special thanks to Owl Rescue Centre NPC for their beautiful idea on owl homes made from recycled plastic material, and for the photograph provided (www.owlrescuecentre.org.za).

## Information on Owl Rescue Centre, Johannesburg

Owl Rescue Centre is a registered non-profit company and permitted rehabilitation facility concerned with the well-being of all owl species in Southern Africa. They are dedicated to protect owls, rescue owls that are in danger and rehabilitate and care for owls that have been injured, are sick, poisoned or orphaned and then release them back into their natural environment using specifically researched release methods. Owl Rescue Centre is also involved in several conservation projects to decrease the high mortality rate of owl species. They have experience in manufacturing Owl Houses, which are made from 100% recycled plastic. This serves as a solution to combat plastic waste. The plastic Owl Houses require no maintenance and will serve many owl generations well. They can be positioned in gardens to ensure safe breeding sites for owls. These Owl Houses act as a solution to the loss of natural habitat and nesting spots in urban development. The Owl Houses are helping to grow the owl population in suburbs, creating a natural solution to rodent control.

Ismail Gani encourages the youth to become involved with centres such as Owl Rescue Centre and to become members of BirdLife Conservation South Africa. He also encourages the youth to become involved in environmental initiatives to recycle plastic bottles, straws, bread plastics, bread tags and bottle tops. All proceeds of this book will go to Owl Rescue Centre South Africa, as well as to Kids Water Foundation for the development of water wells in Limpopo.

Despite Covid-19, Mother Nature continues in the same way everyday and she remains beautiful. Covid-19 has locked human beings in their homes, while Mother Nature recovers without the litter, without the sound pollution and without the smoke. Perhaps Mother Nature is telling human beings to reconsider what they have been doing. Human Beings are not in control and things can't always go the way they plan. We are part of a bigger plan. We have overstepped our limits and we are dependent on something much greater.

The virus is connecting human beings together and is showing us that we are one. This lockdown has made us appreciate the little things that we took for granted. Suddenly the things that we thought were so important are not important at all. Nature has forced us to slow down. The fast-paced, stressful life that had seemed to consume us is lessened. It has made us realize that we are living in a world of excess and luxury. Astonishingly the thing that can protect us most, is a good immune system which can be strengthened with gratitude. This is a loud cry from Nature to wake up. It is time to change our ways. A new journey has begun and a new world will be born.

Ismail Gani

"Earth provides enough to satisfy every man's needs,
but not every man's greed."

Mahatma Gandhi

"The greatest threat to our planet is the belief
that someone else will save it."

Robert Swan

# About the author

**Ismail Gani** is a budding environmentalist and lives in Polokwane, South Africa. He is 17 years old and is already amongst the youngest authors. He has nabbed the title of one of the first to write a children's book about Covid-19 in South Africa. He lives with his parents Rehan and Kaamila and his siblings Faizaan, Ameera, Almaaz and Omar. He has taken advantage of the lockdown by reflecting, reading and practicing his football skills which he is most passionate about. He was inspired during this time to take on the challenge of writing, with the intention to create awareness amongst the youth about conservation and the need to make a change.

Printed in the United States
By Bookmasters